Francis, the Holy Jester

Francis, the Holy Jester

Dario Fo

Translated by

Mario Pirovano

Beautiful
Books

Beautiful Books Limited
36-38 Glasshouse Street
London W1B 5DL
www.beautiful-books.co.uk

ISBN 9781905636716

9 8 7 6 5 4 3 2 1

Francis, the Holy Jester was originally published in Italy under
the title *Lu Santo Giullare Francesco* by Dario Fo, Franca Rame and
Jacopo Fo, in 1999. All illustrations used by kind permission of
the Dario Fo Franca Rame Archive. For all performing rights, please
apply to AGENZIA DANESI TOLNAY, Via Giuseppe Mangili 38A -
00197 Rome, Italy - info@tolnayagency.it.

A catalogue reference for this book is available
from the British Library.

Printed and bound in the UK by CPI Mackays, Chatham ME5 8TD

To Virginia

Good wish

Mario Puzo

This translation is dedicated to Angela

Contents

Translator's note on the text

In order to fully understand and appreciate this translation of Dario Fo's *Lu santo jullare Françesco*, it is important to know that Fo originally wrote and performed it in the vernacular; taking the Lombard dialect of the 13 – 14th Century and, in the manner of the jesters of the day, adding to it primitive Venetian; Umbrian expressions; and onomatopoeic words of all kinds. Franca Rame – actress, collaborator and wife of Dario Fo – then transposed the play into contemporary Italian, and my translation combines aspects of both these versions. Furthermore, over the years, I have directly assisted in numerous presentations of the play performed by Dario Fo, during which he constantly improvised, responding to the audience, location and the times, and so have been able to 'drink from the source'. Thus I have had a unique opportunity to incorporate the best features of the text, through its evolution and enrichment over time, into my translation. Those comparing my translation with the original will find that certain elements of the original have been omitted and others parts appear quite differently in the two versions. However, my modifications do not alter the fundamental nature of the text, nor are they arbitrary. I have maintained an attitude of utmost faithfulness towards the character of the original, seeking to imprint the sentences with the right theatrical rhythm in order to preserve their dramatic strength; and to retain the flavour of the original in the wording. This means some phrasing and usage may appear eccentric, but I hope that this eccentricity will be welcomed and savoured. It is my hope that my translation will offer a deeper insight into Fo's living, growing text, both on the page and the stage.

Mario Pirovano

Editor's note on the text

In preparing the manuscript for publication, I was faced with the challenge of ensuring that readers unfamiliar with the performance, with all its additional physical communication faculties, would clearly perceive both the action, and the identity of each (quoted) speaker. Because of the play's dynamic monologue form, it was decided early on that laying it out according to traditional dramatic conventions would slow things down too much and have a sterilising, stifling effect. Some minor alterations and additions had to be made in order to clarify certain passages, but I worked on the basis of the less interference the better; and worked closely with Mario Pirovano to ensure that as little damage as possible was inflicted on the work. Pirovano and I are both confident that we achieved a good balance.

Anthony Nott

Introduction

(Adapted from a theatrical prologue by Dario Fo)

Francis, the Holy Jester is comprised of episodes from the life of Saint Francis of Assisi that are largely unknown or overlooked, drawn from a variety of historical sources, authentic texts and ancient folk tales of the Umbrian countryside.

I had always thought the label 'jester' was given to Francis by someone of great imagination and subtle humour, and that it was a late nickname, dating perhaps from the 15th or 16th century; the poetic invention of historians and writers. In my research on St. Francis, I discovered – thanks to an absolutely fundamental text by Chiara Frugoni – that Francis had called *himself* a jester; declaring right from the start 'I am God's jester'. At the beginning of the 13th century, to saddle yourself with the label of satirical clown was provocative and dangerous, perhaps even suicidal. The jesters were much loved by the humble people, but hated and persecuted by the powerful, which condemned them to the pillory on every possible occasion. There were even edicts against 'professional clowns', the most famous of which was issued by Frederick the Second of Swabia in 1220. This law was entitled 'Contra Joculatores Obloquentes'. 'Obloquentes' means slanderous, disgraceful, coarse, roguish – it's all there in that word! Also in his edict Frederick incited the people to attack and beat any jesters found at markets or public feasts. And if the beating was excessive, so that one of them died – too bad! There was no problem, because jesters and their friends had no right to appeal to a court of justice, since they were considered unworthy to be classified as civilised human beings. But Francis didn't take the label of jester just to be provocative: he really was a jester. He knew all the tricks of the trade, all the techniques and skills. Witnesses to his harangues, which were the performances of a real jester, assure us that Francis possessed remarkable vocal powers, which allowed him to project his speech to an immense crowd, often more than

5000. And more than that, he expressed himself by moving his arms, his legs and his whole body: 'he made his whole body speak,' wrote a chronicler who attended one of his performances in front of pope Honorius III, who gave Francis's Rule his seal of approval (*Regula bullata*), and who, when he saw him almost dance in his presence, was simultaneously both entertained and moved. On other occasions he began dancing, transforming his sermon into a kind of musical entertainment, a *sirvente* full of lively rhythms, with frequent references to stories of love and passion... all this so he could suddenly change tack and introduce the subject of a *laud* (i.e. a celebratory prayer) of joyful love dedicated to our Creator.

We know of numerous appearances that Francis made in hundreds of cities and townships throughout the Italian peninsular, from the Veneto to Liguria, in the whole of central Italy, and even in the far south. These harangues of his dealt with very diverse themes, but were almost always linked to the tragic conditions of the time which brought suffering, desperation and misery to the whole population of Italy. But in what language did Francis express himself? Dozens of dialects, all mutually incomprehensible, were spoken in Italy at that time. At the beginning of the 13th century there wasn't the least suggestion of an Italian language. The only means of intercommunication was Latin, which only the upper classes knew. But Francis was a genuine jester and knew the composite, flexible language of the story tellers, which successfully drew on idioms from the whole peninsular, idioms full of onomatopoeic sounds, rich metaphors, and always backed up by gestures and by his extraordinary vocal gifts. It really was a *passe-partout* of communication! We know that the disciples and friars who followed Francis in his pilgrimage took notes during all his appearances, indeed they often wrote a description of the whole performance. But of all these documents not one has come down to us. How so? Sadly, forty years after the Saint's death, the new leader of the Franciscan Order, Bonaventura from Bagnoregio, ordered the destruction of all writings on the life of the saint, beginning with Tommaso from Celano's *Leggenda*, which had been written at the command of pope Gregory IX, and, together with that, everything written or dictated by the Saint. In place of all these documents, Bonaventura was appointed by the Chapter General in Narbonne to write the *Leggenda Maggiore*, which, as the new official biography, sterilised the original ideas of the saint and presented them in a sickly sweet manner. At this point we can pretty much say that Francis has been the Saint most 'whitened' by the Church. Documents carrying his beliefs, the new idea of being Christian, were thrown into the flames, as if they were heretical texts. Francis voice has been kept silent for almost five centuries; only around the end of the 17th century, some texts started to re-emerge, saved by those Friars who were passionate advocates of the primal Rule of Francis. Luckily for us, in the last centuries many of the prohibited texts have come back into the light, thanks, above all, to the research done by the same Franciscan friars.

So, as there was no complete historical document to work from, I have boldly allowed myself to reconstruct the stories in the narrative from reports of witnesses and contemporary chronicles. I was not there as your reporter but you must trust me! And I'm sure that when the full original record surfaces – as has happened with so many other writings of Francis's times during the last century – you'll be able to say: 'I've heard it all already!'

Francis, the Holy Jester

THE TIRADE OF FRANCIS AT BOLOGNA, 15th AUGUST 1222

For 30 years, Bologna has been at war with the neighbouring city of Imola. Now, in desperation, the Franciscan brothers of the city have asked Francis to come and try to stop the fighting. Francis addresses the crowd...

'Neapolitans! Here I am! Oh, what gusto, what joy for me to be with you, Neapolitans! Marvellous armed men you are! You jump like ferocious beasts in combat. And how tough you are! When you go to war, to battle, you butcher and kill, shouting on horse-back: "Bump them off! Bump them off! Murder, quarter, spear, behead! Come on, come on! Bravo! Well done!" Neapolitans, good people, courageous, hearty... What? You are not Neapolitans? Where are you from? From the city of Bologna?! All of you? The women too? And what are you doing here in Naples; you of Bologna? Are you travelling through? You are heading to the Holy Land, huh? Are you taking the boat? No? We are not in Naples?! Where are we? Bologna? This is the city of Bologna?! Are you sure...? Oh God! I am staggered! That's why I didn't see the volcano, the great Vesuvius! Nor the sea! I was asking myself: "Where did the sea go?" Ha, ha, we are in Bologna! Ha, ha, ha. This is really funny! What a disaster! Ah, you're right! It's the day after tomorrow that I have to go to Naples! I got it wrong! I'm so confused! I have been practising with a friar in my convent who is from Naples. All day long I talked to him in the Neapolitan dialect. I kept on asking him: "Talk to me in your language! I want to learn it, this fanciful, extravagant language. Speak to me, talk to me, so that when I arrive in Naples I'll make them stand there open-mouthed – ha ha ha – and all the Neapolitans saying: 'Look at him, Francis is speaking like us, Francis the Neapolitan!'" I have made a mistake! I was ready, prepared to talk Neapolitan, but now I'm here in Bologna... I don't speak the Bolognese dialect, not at all. It's a hard language, it's so difficult to articulate. And now, how am I going to work it out? Please, try to be kind, you'll have to give me a hand! You'll have to content yourself with the Neapolitan dialect – pretend that you understand it; show me that you catch every word and even when you don't understand it, pretend you do! Will you? Thank you, thank you, how gentle and generous you are! I love you, I kiss you.

'Bolognese! What lovely people you are! Over-bursting with fierce courage, you fight, you battle, you slaughter each other, crazy with pleasure!

> Fire! A blaze!
> Burn, stick and sink!
> Spear a horse with the lance!
> Slashing the paunches,
> Squashing the bellies!
> Killing and murdering,
> With a sword, with a lance,
> With a mace, with a pike!
> The axe is coming down,
> Deep is the wound!
> *Trucca, tigna, beffa, soffia,*

Dario Fo

zurra, cacchia, ricacchia – TIEH!!!

'Bolognese! How nice you are! Such a long time you have been at war against the people of Imola, that infamous, ugly race! Bitches, beasts, animals they are! So well, so rightly you crush them down, all of them, like mad you clash! What a fight! What a battle! You set half of their city on fire and in revenge they went for your women. I saw a soldier dragging a woman: "Come here!" – "Let me go, let me go, you pig!" And he took her up a tower, and – wooohsplash! Her little child was screaming and yelling, "Mother, mother!" – "Come here, you, little one, and go to see your mum!" – "Eeehhhheee!" – Plaft! Then, at night time, you went with the cavalry and tied long ropes to the door of the main entrance of Imola, you unhinged the door and pulled it down, then you took it to Bologna and set it up in your biggest square as a monument! And those stinkers, those bastards from Imola, with the wind blowing through the city day and night, they all caught a cold – ha ha ha, ha ha! Well done, Bolognese, well done!

6

'Bolognese! How nice you are! Such a long time you have been at war against the people of Imola, that infamous, ugly race! Bitches, beasts, animals they are! And what then? Some rest? A bit of peace? No! You turned against the Emperor, Frederick I, Barbarossa, the Red Beard, that animal of a man who had come to suck the blood of the Lombards – your blood – and nick taxes and tallages. And you chased him and his army out of the region, shouting: "We've had it with you fattening yourself on our meat! Thief!" And by the river Taro, close to the city of Parma, you destroyed his entire army, you unhorsed him! And he, the Emperor – that German! – hid himself under his horse, pretending to be dead. Bravo! Bravo, Bolognese, well done!

'And what then? A bit of peace, some rest? No. Never! The Pope came – Innocent the Third, nicknamed 'The Warrior'. He was raging at the Cathars, the Provençals – those bloody heretics who were going round saying about him, "That one is not the Pope, he's the Antichrist! He only thinks about women, having castles, lands! He's

the Antipope!" They should never have said that!
Pope Innocent the Third had all the saints spinning
around his head; he mounted a horse, charged with
a spear and dragged the French army against the
Albigensians. And you Bolognese, along with the
French, you too mounted your horses and rode
behind him, shouting and chanting and hacking
and slashing:

> Oh oh oh, domine noster – *PRHAFT!!!*
> Christum saeculorum – *SPARSHT!!!*
> Sine die nobis miserere – *ZAC!!!*
> Ahha Alleluja!
> Domine Domine!
> Aaamen!

'And those who didn't go to battle lamented: "Oh,
how lucky they are, fighting, killing, making off with
women! And we, what are we doing? Scratching
our bellies?" Nothing to worry about, even for
those who remained in town there was work to do.
The Lords of Bologna began to snap at each other –
battle cries of "Aiyee!" – The Bonzoni against the

Albergitti! The Camarini against the Zamborghi!
– "Aheee!" – houses burned down, women and
children murdered... In a week 450 dead! All
Bolognese! Such satisfaction, slaughtering within
the family! Such beauty, all these funerals in the
town – one funeral coming down from that road,
another funeral coming from the square, another
from over there – and everybody knew each other,
they were waving: "Oh, look, I killed that one. Of
course, he killed my son." The only moment of
peace! Exult! Cheer! Hurray! Those who went to
fight in Provence are coming back – not all of them,
'cause many have been killed and buried there,
in those foreign fields. Only those who survived
are coming back. But to watch them all marching
proudly – singing with their flags to the wind, and
the trumpets, the drumming – in such martial order,
all strutting, like this... No, no, not quite like that,
because many of them were lame – one with an eye
blinded, another one with a foot chopped off, that
one without a hand – but so proud they were! All
lopsided but proud, marching with their chests out
but leaning a bit to one side: crooked!

'And what then, a bit of peace, some rest? No! Never! Alarm, alarm, alarm! What's happened? The Muslims have robbed the Holy Sepulchre, the holy grave! Innocent the Third, the Pope, called out to the Christians from all over Europe: French, German, English, even from Denmark. They came down through our country, they went down South, to the port of Brindisi, crossed the Mediterranean Sea, arrived in the Palestinian Land with arrows, shields, horses... What a holy massacre! Six thousand killed; dead! Six thousand new graves... to free one empty grave! And when they came back from the Holy Land – a few of them, many more were buried there – they were so proud! They were boasting, showing off and crying out: "I was there on the battlefield! I fought for my country, for my religion and for the flag. I sacrificed myself!" – "Yes, but you must have the mark of war, you must show the wound, the gash! Look at him, he came back from such bloodshed and not a scar, nothing. Hey, how did that happen?" – "Oh, well, I was lucky." – "Lucky? Do me a favour! You've been in a brothel with the whores!" But if someone is marked – hooraaaay! – "My hand? You can see, it's not there! The other hand? I haven't got one." – "Very well, good on you! Bravo! Indeed you have been at war! You are a hero! You are a patriot! Let me shake your hand!" – "But I don't have a hand! Take my foot...!"

'Hoi, women, females, who's crying? Why are you crying? What? You lost your husband?! Where, in Provence? And you? You lost your son? Where, in Palestine? You, your father? So sorry. And you, you lost your husband *and* your lover! I am so sad for you. Ah, I can see so many mothers in grief, so many widows! But you are proud of this widowhood! Yes! You gave your sons, your men, for your country. So honoured you look! So proud...! No? You are not proud?! Woman, what are you saying to me?! You would prefer to have your son embrace you, alive? And you, your husband's head on your chest? You, your father, your brother? You don't care about the glory and the honour?! You too? What? All of you!? Oh God! What a disaster! I have a feeling that you won't listen anymore to

the holy speeches of our notables. You would like to think and to reason with your own brain, with your own head! This is very dangerous! I can already imagine you in a day or two: you will be standing in front of the town hall, asking the Mayor to sign for peace with all the cities and with all the enemies and to impose a perpetual truce even on the families of Bologna! What a disaster! Yes, and you will reach peace. Peace – what a lovely word peeeace is! You fill your mouth with it: peeeace...'
And Francis begins to sing:

> The sun is rising,
> Beautiful and free,
> Then it blazes up,
> High in the sky,
> Till it goes down,
> It goes down...
> The moon comes out,
> Another day is gone.
> The sun is out again,
> It will last
> Till the stars appear,

Appear in the sky.

The peasant is digging,

Then he sows the wheat.

The earth is thirsty,

The wheat can't grow.

Hope it's gonna rain,

Rain, rain, rain…

Tee-tee-tee…

Hey, slow down!

I have said rain,

This is a storm!

The sun is rising again,

The seeds are sprouting,

The girl is in love,

And she gets pregnant...

Now must get married.

Quick, quick, a marriage,

Before the baby is born!

And all in the church,

Din don dun,

The bell is played,

Din don dun.

Everybody

Dance and sing,
Drink and chant!
The sun is rising
The wheat's growing,
The child is getting taller,
Hope he won't go to war.
The sun is rising…
Another day is gone,
Peace, peace, peace…
Peace, peace, peace…

Three days later, the people of Bologna went to the town hall and forced the Mayor and the notables to sign a peace treaty with the town of Imola. This document is known as the *Concilium pacis*, and is still kept in the historical Archives of Bologna today.

THE EXPULSION OF THE ARISTOCRATS AND THE PULLING DOWN OF THE FORTY TOWERS

Many years earlier, when Francis was just 17 years old, he went against his wealthy family, and his entire class, by joining Assisi's rioting masses as they tore down the city's towers and chased off their noble inhabitants. The air rang with shouting...

'Pull, damn it! Pull all together, just like that, good! Come on, let's go! Slacken off a bit now, slacken! Keep on pulling, it's coming down! Be careful, the big tower is collapsing! Watch out, it'll fall on us!' – PTUIMB! PTUAMB! – 'Run everybody! Stones, rocks and blocks are raining down on us!' – PUM! TUA! PUM! BBBUUU! PTOM! POM! PI! – 'Ouch! Right on my foot!' – 'It's down! It's collapsed! Let's go and do another one!' In just one morning they managed to knock down four towers. Now there was the tower of the Mangia family, certainly the toughest one: a high tower stretching right up into the sky. With breathless haste, the rioters begin to tie ropes to the top. Then others rush up the steps, tying one rope here, three ropes there, ten ropes on the opposite side – hundreds and hundreds of ropes tied all around this hunk of a tower – and then they pull: 'Hoy! All together now! Pull on this side! Now you lot on the other side! Now slacken off! Pull! Tug! Heave! No, it's not moving, it's standing erect like a giant cock!' A master mason intervenes: 'No, we can't pull this tower down, it's too tall and its base is too wide. When we pull the ropes, we're just pulling vertically downward. If we pull and tug, all we'll manage to do is drive this huge prick into the ground right up to the roof.' – 'So, how can we do it?' – 'We must pull sideways. Just put a team up the bell-tower next to the Mangia tower and, from there, throw 10 ropes over the massive thing. In this way we'll have one bit of horizontal pull and the rest will be vertical – got it? So, who's for going up to the bell-tower?'

Ten young men together with Francis go up the stairs loaded with hemp ropes. Once they reach the big arches at the top, they throw the ropes over to their comrades across from them, who tie them around the Mangia tower. Francis and the other young men plant themselves firmly: legs apart, with their heels planted on the columns of the arcade. One of the comrades places himself above Francis; another one below – a tangle of legs, columns, feet and taut ropes. 'All together, pull those ropes! Tug at full stretch! And you too, down below. Pull! Heavvvvve…! Whoops!' All of sudden – who knows how it happens – one of Francis's legs slips off the arch and the foot planted against the column slips too – VROM! – He finds himself hurled out of the arcade, hanging onto his rope and heading, like a bolt of lightning, straight for the Mangia tower: 'I'm going to be flattened!' With a desperate twist of his hips, Francis just manages to miss the big tower and he gives a kick to the wall as he passes: 'Safe!' Clinging to the rope, he swings round the big tower, around and around. Someone cries: 'Hey, enjoying the ride, eh?!' With each turn, the rope knots around the big tower, tightens, gets shorter and shorter: 'God! I'm going to get smashed!' Another kick, and he turns back again, going backwards. The rope unwinds: 'Heeeelp! Make way! Damn, I'm coming back… toward the steeple… the bells…!' – VRUHOM! – He slips into the steeple's arch, right inside the big bell! – BLUM! – He grabs the clapper that dongs loudly – BLUM! BLIUM! BLIUM! DON! DON! DON! – 'My head! God, what a bang on the head!' – DIN! DON! – He becomes the clapper! – DON! DON! – The other bells begin to chime – DIN! DIN! DON! DON! DEN! DON! DIN! DON! DON! – PLAFF! – 'My heaaad!' When his comrades finally pull him out of the niche, poor Francis is all crooked. One of them holds up his head while another straightens out his legs. 'How are you doing?' – 'I'm all right.' – 'Now, can you go down the stairs by yourself…? Careful – there are two hundred and fifty steps… watch out!' He begins to go down slowly; he falters, and – TON! TON! TON! DIN! DIN! TON! TON! TROTOTOTON! SLAFF! – He reaches the bottom, all twisted up like a ball of rags. They pick him up and try to untangle him – he has one leg around his neck, the other one under his armpit, one arm twisted behind his back: 'Pull!' – 'No, that leg is mine!' In the end, there he is, all in one piece, on his feet. They try to get him to move but it's as though he's set in plaster. Four of them shoulder him and take him home. As soon as his mother sees him, she cries: 'Oh…! My son is deaaad! Ihiiiiiiiiii!' – 'Mother… please… do not scream… I have twelve bells in my brain!' They carry him down to the cellar, down next to the wine: 'Silence! Not a word!' Some poor soul passing by yells loudly: 'Franciiis! How is it going?' – 'Aggghhhhh! Quiet! Please!'

So, there he remains for seven days: still; stuck; in complete silence. When he comes out he looks a bit tipsy; bewildered; he walks crookedly. On meeting him, his teasing comrades say: 'Hey, Francis, did you already strike the hour? Come on, ring the morning bell!' And he, like a good sport, plays along, going: 'DIN! DAN!' Because Francis was a spirited fellow, and spiritual too.

But I must say it was his 'dearest friends' who

badmouthed Francis the most. Many years later, soon after he had become a Saint, everybody everywhere on earth, across the seas and beyond the mountains, knew about his beatitude and they – these nasty 'friends' – were going around saying: 'I remember when Francis was flooded by divine Grace, it was the day he got banged on the head inside the great bell. After this big bang, he was not the same anymore. He was going around all dazed: face up, as if he were stunned, always looking at the sky, at the birds and also at the moon. He said to the moon: "Hello, sister!" then to the stars: "Little sisters…", to the sun: "Hello, brother", to the earth: "Mother earth." All one family! Then he was speaking with the animals, with the birds, with the horses, the wolves and even the ants, saying: "Nice little ants, sweet little animals… little beasts all in a line, orderly… *trillilli li lirili*…" Then he blessed them, and walked off… forgetting the little ants and stomping all over them!

FRANCIS MEETS THE WOLF IN GUBBIO

One day, Francis is on his way to Gubbio, to meet his companions, when he hears some peasants screaming...

'Help! God save us! The slaughterer is here! Run away! Every man for himself – he's coming!' – 'What's happening? Who are you fleeing? Who is after you?' – 'The wolf from Gubbio! A monster! A lion!' – 'Oh, a lion! Don't exaggerate!' – 'I don't know anything about lions, but – damn! – that face looks like a crocodile! He opens his jaws wide in front of you... With a single bite he tore a lamb apart! He seized a dog with his jaws and chopped it up like meat for stuffing. What a fright! When he shows you his fangs, and his tremendous eyes, it curdles your blood!' – 'Hoi, you might not know much about lions, but with crocodiles you're part of the family! You said that he's after you, but I don't see a wolf! Tell me, where is this beast approaching from?' – 'Over there, Francis – there, he's coming down the hill on the other side of the valley!' – 'But he's only small!' – 'It is a matter of perspective. Wait till he gets near and you'll see.' – 'Well, I'd like to go and meet him.' But Francis's brothers say: 'Dear Francis, please, calm down a moment. You've gone crazy: first you embrace the lepers, then you strip off naked in the church and now you want to talk to wolves! Why don't you just write it a letter instead?' – 'No, I want to speak to him personally!' And Francis goes down the hill into the valley. Meanwhile, all the people – peasants, shepherds, women, and children – have gone up to the ridge, as if they were at the theatre, saying: 'Let's watch this meeting of Francis with the wolf!' Francis comes down the slope and from around a hump ahead of him, the wolf appears again. 'Bah, there's nothing to be frightened of, in fact he looks rather little to me!' – 'It is a question of distance! Wait till he reaches you!' The wolf comes forward… comes down… and they meet below the hump. When they are six steps from each other, Francis exclaims: 'What a beast! Good heavens, how big he is! And what fangs! He really does look

Francis addressing the Bolognese

The destruction of the towers

The wolf of Gubbio terrorising the peasants

Francis meeting with Pope Innocent III

Francis embracing the pigs

Francis preaching to the birds

Francis and his brothers at the spring

Francis dying in the Porziuncola

like a lion. I might just write him a letter and say ciao!' At the top of the ridge someone is betting: 'Now watch, another step... the wolf will jump on Francis and devour him!' The wolf approaches Francis, getting closer and closer. When he's right in front of Francis – wonder! – he slowly crouches down on his paws, like a farm dog, bends his head and rests his jaws between Francis's feet. Francis begins to talk to the wolf: 'Now then, wolf, what's the matter with you? Eh? Do you think that these are nice things to do? Answer me!' The peasants above the hillock are shouting: 'Hey, speak up! We can't hear a damned thing!' – 'Oh, be quiet! This is a private conversation – intimate! Now then, wolf, would you like to tell me what's got into your head? You go around tearing up dogs and sheep and you don't even taste them; it's just for the pleasure of tearing out their bowels, of striking terror, eh? Come on, speak up, I'm talking to you.' – 'Oh, well, I *na, give, up, or scac hotorn, lave ne...*' – 'Hey, you, wolf, don't play games with me! Speak properly!' – 'Oh, yes, it's true, I like biting, jumping on sheep, tearing away their bowels and spreading them all around… to see people running away and screaming in terror… ha, ha, ha!' – 'And do you think this is nice… eh?' – 'What else can I do? That's my nature. It's my natural behaviour!' – 'Oh, that's a good excuse! Nature! Did you think of that all by yourself? Did you come up with that? Now it is all nature's fault! If someone is born with the nature of a thief, he can steal! A rapist, he can rape women! Slaughtering, lying, killing – it is all nature's fault! All must allow it! Woe betide he who dares breathe against it! Woe betide he who becomes indignant! It's nature's fault! And those who are lacking in nature – the poor, the ragged people – always blows to their heads, kicks up their asses and spit in their eyes! This is what they deserve! On your knees, bend your head…! No, no, my dear wolf. It's not honest!' – 'Well, what's it got to do with me? Blame the Eternal Father! It's he who made me this way.' – 'But what a way to live is this? What kind of a life…? Answer!' – 'Yes, you're quite right, Francis: it really is a dog's life, looking at it from a wolf's point of view. I really would like to live like a good beast – more gentle – and I did try, Francis, I have even tried to eat vegetables and roots, but after a week I had such diarrhoea! I was shitting all over the place. I really would like to be good. If you help me, Francis, I am ready to change my life!' – 'You are? Are you prepared to do so? Swear on it! Are you going to swear?' – 'Yes, I do. I agree!' – 'Hey, you, up there, peasants, brothers! The wolf has agreed to change his life. He is going to be good, but you must help him: take him with you into your community. You only need to feed him. You can throw him the leftovers, the same that you give to your dogs: the wolf eats, the dogs eat and everyone is at peace! What do you say?' – 'Fine, but what are we going to get out of it?' – 'For a start he will not maul you! Then, once he's got a good reputation, he can guard you from the other wolves and even from the brigands and murderers who are always after you. Don't worry: he will earn his living. So, wolf, do you agree? Are we going to enter into this contract? Don't make me cut a poor figure. And you, peasants, are you convinced? Shall we go ahead with this deal? Well then! I'm coming up to introduce you: this is the wolf; they are the peasants. Aren't you going to shake hands? No, there's no need of this ritual. Go on then, off you go.' They form a procession: the wolf in the middle, the peasants and the women around him, all walking at the same pace. 'Be careful,' – Francis calls after them – 'don't tread on his toes, 'cause I'll tell you for nothing he will savage you!' The kids are last, at the back of the line. Everyone disappears, leaving Francis and his brothers alone. 'Well, this wolf matter is settled! Now let's go to the quarry in Stroppiano to get our stones!'

They set off up the mountain and reach the quarry the following day. The quarrymen, who dig out the marble slabs, immediately recognize Francis – they know he is a bricklayer and greet him: 'Hey, Francis it's good to see you. They say you have been repairing churches! How are you getting on?' – 'It's going all right, but I have run out of stones – I need three or four cartfuls!' – 'I am sorry, Francis, but unfortunately nobody can take away stones, slabs or blocks anymore.' – 'Why not? Doesn't the cave belong to the municipality?'

– 'Well, it did.' – 'What's happened?' – 'The monks – the Celestian[1] – those from Civitella; their monastery was hit by an earthquake, so they went to the Pope and asked him: "Holy Father, a sidewall of our monastery has collapsed. We need to dig out stones from the Stroppiano quarry. Can you give us the privilege to be the only ones allowed to take away stones for a week?" – "All right," said the Pope, "if it is only for a week, I give you this privilege." On their way back home, the Pope died and the monks went around saying: "The quarry is ours. The Pope gave us the privilege for good."' Francis becomes red; filled with anger: 'Those wicked people, they cheated the Pope even on his deathbed! I am going right away to speak to these Celestian monks.' Francis's companions try to hold him back: 'Francis, calm down! This morning you worked in the fields, then you spoke to the wolf, now you want to go to the Celestian monks – don't be so eager, let it drop! Watch out, Francis, these

---

[1] Not to be confused with the 'Celestine' order, which began in 1264, so did not exist in Francis's time. According to local (Umbrian) popular belief, the Celestian monks go back to the beginning of Christianity, and were considered heretics in the 5th century.

Celestian monks are pretty cocky! And the prior, when he sees you arriving in rags looking like a beggar, he will loose the dogs on you – such fearful beasts!' – 'Dogs, against me? What can dogs do to me? To one who talks to the wolves!? Listen: if you are afraid, I'll go to the monastery alone. You wait for me here, at Stroppiano.'

So Francis goes alone. He arrives at the monastery, and in front of the main door he takes hold of the doorknocker, lifts it up, and bangs it on the door: BODON! No one comes. Again he lifts up the doorknocker: BODON! – 'Niaaaaa!!! Ooouuch!' – He forgot to take his hand away! As he screams, the guardian comes out onto the highest arcade. 'Who is shouting at this time of the night?' – 'It's me, Francis. I need…' – 'I know what you need, ragged as you are: food! You're looking for food. I'm sorry, it's too late: there is no bread left. Come back tomorrow!' – 'No, no, please! I don't want bread, but stones!' – 'Stones? Have you come here at this hour of the night to take the piss? Get lost! Otherwise I'll give the stones to you but all on your head!' – 'No, I won't go away! I need to speak personally to the Prior!' Francis pushes against the door with his shoulder and it gives way. Then he slips into the portico shouting: 'Prior, father Prior!' On the tallest tower appears the Head Monk. 'Who is it? Who is calling me?' – 'It's me, Francis! I need to get stones from the quarry!' – 'Ah, I know you, you're that madcap from Assisi! You strip naked in the church, you steal money from your father and give it to tramps just like yourself! You embrace lepers! You are also infective! Get out, or I'll set the dogs on you!' – 'No, I cannot go away. It was the Lord Jesus Christ in person who ordered me: "Go and save my church!", he said' – 'Get the dogs onto him!' Two servants appear, dragged in by two wild beasts, which they unleash. Francis tries to turn but the dogs are upon him; they seize his buttocks – those tiny, skinny buttocks of his – 'Oihoihh! Ooouuch!' – and begin savaging him. Suddenly, Francis sees a black shadow pounce on the mastiffs and hears a wild roaring: 'Ohahuhehah!' There's a big fight and the two mastiffs flee, crying: 'Kaiiikaiiiikaiikaiiii!!!' – 'But what's this black shadow? Hoi! Is it you, the wolf from Gubbio?' – 'Yes, it's me!' – 'And what are you doing around here?' – 'Oh, I was just passing by and I heard you screaming; I recognised your voice and I came in to give the dogs a good bite!' – 'Well done! You did very well; I was having some problems with those animals. Listen to me, wolf: it's best if we get out of here immediately because the Prior is even worse than his dogs. Let's go!' And off they go up the slope. Francis asks: 'Tell me, wolf, didn't you feel good at Gubbio, with all those peasants feeding you?' – 'Oh yes, Francis, I did. At first it was great: they treated me really well, giving me food, caressing me; they even deloused me! Then – and I don't know how it happened – they began to be disrespectful. They spat on me, they kicked me; not to talk about the food – slop! vomit! – even the pigs wouldn't eat it! The kids threw stones at me… One day, while I was sleeping, they tied some straw to my tail and set it on fire! Look at it, it's all burned! What a tail! I am so ashamed that when I meet someone, I hide it between my legs! In the end I ran away! You know, Francis, I understood one thing: if someone is born a wolf, he must remain a wolf; because if you forget to bite, and grind your teeth, and terrorise with your voice; nobody respects you: they take you for a fool and they piss on you!' – 'Yeah, you're damned right, wolf. And it was my fault. I was so presumptuous! I tried to turn animals into good men; I should have tried to turn men into good animals!'

FRANCIS GOES TO THE POPE IN ROME

Another time, Francis is again striding along on the road to Gubbio. He's walking through the village of Beast, near Bastard, when all of a sudden he hears voices calling out his name...

Some young men walk up, smiling, and say to him: 'Hey! Francis! How wonderful that we've found you! We were searching for you!' – 'What for?' – 'There's a wedding, here. It's the marriage of one of our friends and a girl so sweet that she looks like spring. How young they are! You should see them both! You must come and greet them and cheer the feast with one of your stories, perhaps one from the Gospel. It would be so great to listen to you!' – 'I can't. I am sorry. My companions are waiting for me!' – 'But just one story! Come on, Francis, please!' – 'No, I can't, I've got to go.' – 'Just a glass of wine with us!' – 'Oh, well! If it's for a glass of wine...'

They arrive at the marriage feast. The guests greet and embrace him: 'Francis, how good to see you, sit down! Have a drop of wine, have a nice piece of roast, eat!' Everybody drinks a toast to the bride, who is crying with joy. Her mother too is crying. A voice cries out: 'If we carry on like this, we'll sprinkle the whole table with tears. Come on, Francis, stop all this! Put an end to all this whining, tell us a story!' Francis stands up and begins: 'All right, I will try to tell you a story, and rightly from the Gospel. And since this is a wedding, I will tell you the tale of the Wedding at Caana...

'The situation was just as it is here: the bride was crying, the mother weeping, the father grumbling, and none of the guests were seated at the table. Someone asks: "What's going on? Has the groom run away?" Another one replies: "No, no, the groom is swearing like a trooper!" – "What's happened then?" – "There's been an accident: they've run out of wine." – "What a disaster! – *a bride wet with wine is a lucky bride...* But wet with water is a curse, a misfortune, a danger to flee!" At that moment a young man came in. His name was Jesus. Christ was his nickname. He wasn't alone; he was with his mother – a wonderful woman known as The Madonna. They were guests – highly regarded – arriving a few minutes late. At this stage, the man pouring the wine walked up to The Madonna and said: "Madonna, dear, can you help us? We've run out of wine!" – "Run out of wine? Why have you bought so little?" – "So little? We bought enough wine for three weddings but these people don't drink wine; they guzzle it! Please, Madonna, help us!" – "But I don't know anything about wine! You should go to my son Jesus – he knows a bit about wine." As soon as the wine pourer approached him, Jesus said: "Yes, yes, I've heard you are running out of wine, but I've never done a 'wine miracle.'" – "Well, can we try one?" – "Yes, we can try. I can't guarantee you anything, but we can try. All right, have you got some water?" – "Water? We've got all the water you like. Did you see, when you came to the house, just before you entered the door? There are seven vessels of water. As you know, we not only wash our hands before the feast, but also our feet: *Clean feet before the feast refreshes brain and spirit*. There are even some louts that go straight into the bucket with their shoes on!" – "All right! Bring me the water, please." – "But, Jesus, you're not going to make wine with *that* water, are you? It has such an unpleasant smell!" – "Excuse me, but when you make wine what do you do?" – "We take the grapes..." – "And then?" – "We put the grapes into a vat..." – "And then?" – "We climb into the vat and tread the grapes with our feet..." – "So, feet before or feet afterwards – isn't it the same thing?" – "...Oh, yes, I didn't think about that." At this point the Messiah raises his right hand to the sky, then he takes the fingers one by one and pulls and pops them. Then he holds up three fingers – only three, the other two are held tight against the palm – and makes a sign over the water which the guests don't understand: it's the sign of the cross, but nobody understands it because they don't know that Jesus will end up nailed to the cross. Then the water in the vessels begins to quiver... changes colour... becomes red... boils... and, as clouds of pink vapour rise from the bottom, the smell of crushed grapes spreads all around – enough to make you drunk! Someone staggers by, already drunk. Someone who is dying of thirst picks up a small mug and dips it into this new wine. "Stop it, for Christ's sake!" says Jesus, "It's hot, you'll burn yourself. Let it cool down a little!" And it is wine; what wine! Ye blessed in purgatory! Mellow, a little bitter in the middle, a little salty at the back, a bit sharp – at least three years old, a golden vintage! Jesus gets up onto a table and begins pouring wine for everybody: "Drink, good people, be happy, be mirthful, do not wait for heaven tomorrow! Today, here, on this earth, is heaven!" Then he meets his mother's eyes: "Forgive me mother, I am a little drunk." Everybody raises his cup: "Bravo, Jesus, well done, Jesus! Bravo Jesus! Jesus, you are divine! Or perhaps I should I say 'di-*wine*'!" '

A priest nearby comes forward: 'Francis, how wonderful you are, how good you are at telling stories! I have never heard the Gospel told in such a way. How funny you are – a real jester! But, excuse me, I have to ask you something… only to help you... Tell me, Francis, do you have permission to tell the Gospel in public? In the vulgar tongue, too? In this way?' – 'Why? Do I need permission?' – 'Oh blissful innocence! But certainly you need permission, for you are not a priest. It is a mortal sin! It is not possible. Beware Francis, when you go around preaching; be careful: those of the Holy Inquisition are always around, they wouldn't think twice about burning you at the stake!' – 'Crikey! So what should I do?' – 'You should go and ask for permission from the Bishop, or the Cardinal, or – best of all – from the Pope.' – 'The Pope?' – 'Yes, the Pope.' – 'Heavens! I didn't know... Well, at this point let me just say that I am sorry... I must leave. Thank you, thank you, dear priest. Goodbye, cheers to all of you, wish the newly-weds happiness and enjoyment from me. Thank you all. I have got to go, my lovely friends. I kiss you dearly!'

And off he goes, sad, running to where his companions are waiting for him. When they see him they cry out: 'Francis, what's happening?' – 'Nothing. It's alright.' – 'Nothing? You look like a beaten dog!' – 'Brothers, we can't go around telling the Gospel anymore.' – 'What? Why not?' – 'We need permission.' – 'Permission?' – 'Yes, permission. We have to be careful when we go around preaching: there are those of the Holy Inquisition who don't think twice about burning people at the stake. We must go to the Pope to ask for permission, and while we are there, we can state our idea of Community!' – 'To the Pope?' – 'Yes, the Pope.' – 'Oh, well, that's easy: we go down to Rome with our hands in our pockets and say: "Hey, here we are, Pope, we've arrived".' – 'And why not? He's not going to eat us!' – 'You never know...'

So off they went, four friars and Francis, step by step, crossing the Tevere Valley, heading for Rome. After a week's walking, they enter Rome and ask: 'Excuse me, where is the Pope's Palace?' – 'Go down that road, turn left, then cross the bridge over the river, pass through that little valley, turn right, go up till you are in front of a big palace. Behind it, there is another big palace with a lot of windows. Inside there, I don't know in which window, there is the Pope.' – 'Thank you.' They go on walking, they arrive, and, when they are in front of the Palace, a row of guards stands in their way: 'Stop where you are. What do you want?' – 'I am Francis, I have come from Assisi. I need to talk to the Pope.' – 'You think it's that easy to speak to the Pope!? You want an audience? First of all you'll have to write a request, possibly in Latin.' – 'But I don't remember Latin.' – 'Then write it as you like. The important thing is that you must be patient – very patient! Because patience is not only the virtue of the saints, but also of those tramps and wretches who own nothing, like you!' – 'Oh, thank you very much!' Francis writes a little note and hands it to the guard, who enters the palace.

Francis and his companions sit down in the square and wait all day long. Evening comes, then night, then morning. Another day passes, and nobody shows up; nobody comes to call them. At this point Francis says: 'He's taking his time...!' – then he hits his forehead – 'Oh, how stupid, how boneheaded I am! I didn't think of it! Here, in Rome, lives a

dear friend of mine! Colonna, Cardinal Colonna
– he's the Pope's Counsellor! Such a good man;
a holy man! His name is Giovanni. We must find
him, quick, let's look for him.' They ask around:
'Excuse me, please, where is the house of Cardinal
Giovanni Colonna?' – 'The Cardinal? Go down
that road, turn right, go straight on for 200 metres
and turn right again, go over a bridge and turn left,
and there is a square, on the corner of that square
there is a big palace with a lot of windows – that's
Colonna's house.' – 'Thank you.' And off they go.

They arrive in front of the Cardinal's house. They
try to enter the Palace but immediately the guards
stop them: 'Where do you think you are going?'
– 'To see Cardinal Colonna!' – 'First you have to
write a request.' – 'Ha, here we go again!' At that
moment Cardinal Colonna is just getting dressed, he
looks down through the window and sees Francis.
'Franciiis!! Is that you?' – 'Oh, Colonna! Colonna,
come down!' – 'Stay there, Francis, don't move.
I'm coming right down!' Colonna runs quickly
down the winding staircase. He runs round and

round, and when he reaches the bottom he has to make a half-turn back the other way to stop himself spinning: 'Oh Francis, what a pleasure to embrace you! Let me take a look at you. You look like a thief, so ragged you are! What are you doing here in Rome?' – 'Oh, Colonna, I need your help: I came with my brothers to talk to the Pope.' – 'The Pope? This Pope?' – 'Yes, why, do you have another one?' – 'No, no, we have only this one, for now, but he's so haughty; so hoity-toity…' – 'Please, I need to talk to him.' – 'All right, Francis, I'll see what I can do. But now, please, go to my house for some rest.' – and, to the guards – 'Take these dear friends of mine to my palace, give them something to eat and get them to have a wash; to change their clothes,' – and, whispering – *'they smell – you can't go near them!'* – 'Thank you so much, Colonna.' – 'Now go, Francis, I'll see you later on.'

Cardinal Colonna runs off to the Pope's palace, goes up the stairs and enters the hall. The Pope is sitting there on his golden throne with a book in his hands, reading. 'Oh dear Innocent…' – Colonna is very familiar with the Pope, and just calls him Innocent without the number. 'Colonna, tell me, what is it that you want?' – 'A friend of mine – Francis is his name – has just arrived from Assisi. He would like to talk to you.' – 'You said Francis?' – 'Yes, Francis.' – 'By chance, is he one of those who sat under the arcade from yesterday afternoon until this morning?' – 'Yes, Francis is one of them.' – 'And, I ask you: this Francis, by chance, does he have a smile?' – 'Yes, Francis has a smile.' – 'I do not like him.' – 'But why not? Francis is a good man; a fine man!' – 'I do not like him. I do not like those who have a smile.' – 'But Francis is a nice man, he's kind, he loves the Church…' – 'I don't care, I do not like those who smile! Do you remember that one – Pietro Valdo was his name – that mad wretch who came from Provence? He too had the same smile. Do you remember the Waldensians, those heretics? What a war they drove me to wage against them, I had to slaughter Christians like lambs at Holy Easter! I still have nightmares today – I wake up with my hands covered with blood! I don't want to risk another war like that one right here in Rome! I don't want to see him! Throw him out!' – 'Hey, calm down, Innocent, don't get nervous. All right, I'll send him away. Good-bye, I salute you, Innocent... the Third!' And off he goes running home, where Francis is waiting: 'I'm sorry, Francis, I don't know what to say... but the Pope has all the Bishops spinning around his head; he's having fits! Let's wait for another day.'

That evening Francis and the others cannot eat. They cannot sleep either. And the Pope too goes to bed without a meal. And he too cannot sleep – he is shaking, sweating with a fever, and in the middle of the night he has a terrifying nightmare: he is inside a big cathedral and all of a sudden the columns start trembling. The arches are breaking up: stones, bricks, dust everywhere; the floor is opening up – an earthquake! Just at that moment a little man appears, dressed in rags, and – ZAP! – with one hand, he stops a column from falling, then – ZHAK! – he raises a foot and stops another one. Then he raises his arms, which stretch impossibly up, and stops the main arch and, with one foot here, one foot there, he secures everything. All stopped! Silence!! Innocent wakes up in a sweat. He is trembling all over. He calls the guard: 'Go and get Colonna, my Counsellor. Bring Cardinal Colonna here, quickly! Hurry up!' And off he goes to Colonna's house and shouts: 'Colonna, it's me: the Guard! Innocent wants to see you right away! Come down!' Colonna runs down the stairs and sets off towards the Pope's palace – Colonna, the 'Running Cardinal'! – and when he arrives he asks the Pope: 'Innocent, what's happening?' – 'Colonna, I had a horrible dream, a nightmare, but it was so real! I found myself under the main arch of the church and it was falling on me! The columns; the arches were coming down, and the floor was opening under my feet, when a little man appeared. Then he stretched out his arms and legs and stopped the columns and the cupola from falling! He stopped everything!' – 'Well then, it's all going to be fine!' – 'No, Colonna, I know, a catastrophe is going to befall us!' – 'No, no, come on! We'll be fine. But… tell me, Innocent: what was he like? Who did he look like; the little man that you saw?' – 'I don't know, I was so upset!' – 'Didn't you see his face? How was he dressed?' – 'I can't remember.' – 'But, listen, Innocent: by chance, did he have a smile?' – 'Yes… now that you mention it, I remember: he had a smile.' – 'Innocent! That was Francis! It was God himself that put this dream into your head: he wants you to meet Francis.' – 'The suspicion did cross my mind... Please, Colonna, go and get him, bring him here, I want to talk to him. Please, go!' – 'Yes, I'll go right away, Innocent!' Colonna rushes back to his house and cries: 'Francis, exult! The Pope – he wants to see you. Let's go everybody, quick, he's waiting for you. But please, Francis, hold your smile.'

When they arrive, the Pope points his finger at him and asks: 'Are you Francis?' – 'It's me, Holy Father. I am Francis.' – 'Very well. Now, please, Colonna, leave me alone with him. And you too, brothers, leave, please.' Off they go and the Pope continues: 'Now, Francis. You have asked for me. Tell me, Francis, what is it that you want? Just ask me and, if I can, I will give it to you.' – 'Oh, Holy

Father, how marvellous you are! You ask me to ask you, and, if you can, you are going to give to me what I ask for. Oh, thank you, Holy Father! I would like to go around telling the Gospel in the vulgar language, in the vernacular, with no interpretation, without a comma and without gloss. I would like to go and tell the Gospel in the market square; in the streets; where people work; in the fields; in the taverns.' – 'And in the churches? Never?' – 'I would like to go to the churches too, Holy Father, but the priests are already there. We would just make too much confusion.' – 'You are right there, Francis. And what else do you ask? Ask me, Francis, and, if I can, I will give it to you.' – 'Oh, Holy Father, how magnificent you are! I would like to have your permission to build up a Community, and a 'Rule', in which everybody is equal and loves each other and everybody lives in poverty and follows the Gospel as it is written.' – 'Well, I like the idea. And what else?' – 'I would like all of us to join together but without any money: the first rule of our Rule will be that nobody shall have possessions, houses or land! We'll go around without bags; with no carts; without pockets; nothing to carry. We won't need homes to go to. We will help the peasants in the fields to earn our living.' – 'That's nice. I like it... everyone without goods... But the Community; can the Community have possessions?' – 'No, of course not!' – 'But how will you survive? If there is a bad season or a famine and there is no food left, what are you going to do?' – 'We trust in Holy Providence! After all did He, our Lord Jesus, go around with bags or with a cart? Did he go around carrying money or asking for it? No, He did not!' – 'Oh, yes, it's true: that one – a right mad one – he and the other twelve like him; quite crazy the whole lot! But you forget one detail about him, one small detail: that He, Jesus, was the Son of God, and He was the Father too, and the Holy Spirit, all together: Son of God, Father and Holy Spirit! No one understood how He did it. He was the kind of guy that, for example, when he went around with his disciples, everyone followed him for days and days, and when he settled up in the mountains, everyone sat around him drinking the words from his lips and when someone beside him fainted onto the ground, Jesus asked: "What's happening?" – "Well, Jesus, we haven't eaten all day." – "So, what are we waiting for? Let's eat. Stop everybody, let's eat!" – "Yes, but, Jesus, we didn't bring anything." Those Palestinians were so disorganised! But Jesus was not discouraged and asked: "Is there anyone here who has some bread?" – "Yes, I have a loaf of bread!" – "Please, give it to me." Jesus broke it into pieces and put it in a basket. "Is there anyone here who's got some cheese; dry meat; salami?" – "No, we haven't got any of those." Then, from the far end of the group, a voice rang out loud: "I have a fish!" Can you imagine someone up a mountain for three days with a fish in his pocket? Anyway, Jesus took the fish, broke it into small pieces, and threw it into the basket. Then he lifted up the basket, shook it and tossed everything up in the air. A cascade of sandwiches came down! Slices of bread filled with fish wrapped with salad, the fish without any bones and everything held in place with a toothpick! "Hurrah, hurrah, bravo Jesus!" Everybody ate with great joy. "What a meal! What a feast! Jesus, what a lovely religion is this!'"

At this point, Francis bursts out laughing: 'Ha, ha, Holy Father, you are the real jester, you are the storyteller, not me! But by saying this, Holy Father, you mean that, since not one of us is able to perform miracles, there's no point in trying to start this Community. Let's leave it, it's not going to work.' – 'But no, Francis, wait! Don't be so narrow-minded! Don't be so square-minded! There is still the dialectic!' – 'I don't understand, Holy Father. What do you mean?' – 'Oh, my dear Francis, look at you, the way you are: always wearing a smile, and so charming you are that when you meet someone he will say: "Look here Francis, I have so many cows, here, Francis, take this heifer, it's for you and your friends." And you, Francis, can take the heifer and put it with your provisions! Along comes another one: "Here, Francis, I have so many houses! Take one for yourself, Francis. Keep this house for you and your friends." And there is someone else that says: "Here, Francis, I have a lot of money, it's falling out of my pockets. Take this money, Francis, for you and your companions." And you, Francis, can take the money! After all, where does the word "Providence" come from? "Providence" – from "provisions"!' – 'No,' – says Francis – 'it is not possible. You see, Holy Father, when you take goods and store them, and then distribute them to the poor or to those in need; that is the greatest power of all – greater, even, than the power of the Emperor! The power of Charity! It's like this, Holy Father: you are poor? Here, take this heifer, it's for you, take it home. And you, too, are poor: this house is for you, take it. And you, here, take this money! And you? No, not you! I know that you're a poor man but I don't like you and I won't give you anything. It is an injustice? I don't care. I'm the one that decides on the shares! It's me that gives out the stuff! Because I have the power of Charity!' – 'The power of Charity? You are telling this to *me?* To *ME!?* I, who am here, sitting on a High Backed chair! To me, dressed with diamonds, rings, gold – you are telling this to me, who owns castles and palaces? I have soldiers, I have prisons and I make laws. I send soldiers against those who step on my feet – I stamp on their heads!!! *Non sum dignus*? You are telling me that I don't have a right to all this?! Oh, now I find out who you *really* are, Francis! You are worse than Pietro Valdo, the heretic, you are... Ah, ah, I am sick... please, forgive me, Francis, forgive me, but I can't understand what you are saying. Or, rather, I do understand it, but I cannot accept it. Even people like me understand but they cannot accept. But I know who you can tell these things to: you must go into a pigsty and tell these things to the pigs! Yes, Francis, go to the pigs, talk to them, they will listen to you and they will understand you. Go, Francis! Go! Go!' – 'Oh, thank you, Holy Father, for this advice!' Francis goes out into the courtyard and calls his companions: 'Brothers, let's go! The Pope gave me the wonderful advice to speak to the pigs. Let's go!'

They leave the city and set off to the countryside. When they get to the fields, Francis says: 'There is a big pigsty over there. Wait for me here, I'll go alone.' As he enters, he is faced with a fat grunting sow with many boobs. Behind it is a huge oinking male pig and all the other pigs in the family. 'My splendid pigs! Brothers!' – says Francis, with outstretched arms – 'I came here by order of the Pope, who has convinced me to talk to you about the Gospel, Charity and the love that we should have for each other!' The pigs look at Francis with their eyes wide open. Francis kisses the pigs, embraces them, and rolls in the shitty mud with them. Then, all covered in pig shit, he runs toward the city with his shocked companions following behind. When they arrive at the Pope's Palace, the guards sniff the air... and disappear. Francis enters the palace, goes up the stairs and enters the main hall. The Pope is seated at the dinner table with some very distinguished persons – noblewomen, princes and Cardinals – who are all eating, conversing, laughing and raising their glasses. When Francis appears, a woman says: 'God, it stinks in here! Where is that stench coming from?' Francis walks, smiling, towards Innocent. 'Marvellous Pope! Thank you for the great gift you have given me! I went where you ordered me to go: among the pigs. How wonderful! I have embraced them, I have rolled around in the dung with them, and they have listened to me.

Thank you so much, I am so happy! Holy Father, thank you.' Francis is out of his mind with joy; he is dancing and jumping; he gets a bit carried away and does a big twirl and – splat! – shit flies all over the place. A woman throws up. Innocent raises his arm to command the guards to seize Francis, but Colonna, Cardinal Colonna, grabs his arm. 'What are you doing, Innocent? What do you want to do? Do you want to arrest him; throw him into prison? Be careful, Innocent, Francis is not alone: he has brothers and sisters; he is father and mother of thousands and thousands of people.' – 'Yes, but he…' – 'It's your fault. You provoked him and he went. What are you going to do, Innocent? Beat him up? Kill him? Well, do it if you like; do it! You will see what will happen! The war against Pietro Valdo will look like a walk in the country! The sea will turn to blood, the mountains will fall and crush Rome – you will see! Do it if you like! Do it!' – 'And what am I supposed to do?' – 'Forgive him! Forgive him and embrace him!' – 'Embrace him? But he's covered in shit!' – 'That's because of you!' Innocent walks towards Francis, embraces him and hugs him to his bosom: 'Francis, forgive me! Forgive me, for I did not understand the wonderful folly of your mind.' Then he addresses all those in the hall: 'Now listen to me, you princes, Cardinals and Bishops. From this moment on, I grant Francis, and his companions, the right to go around and preach as he likes, as he wants. He can tell the Gospels wherever he chooses, and he and his people can also live on charity. Go, Francis, go. I give you permission for your Rule – orally for now, and later I'll give it to you in writing.' – 'Oh, Holy Father, thank you, thank you! Brothers, we have permission! The Holy Father gave us permission! Let's go!'

They all run out and arrive in a square where there is a market. Francis jumps up on a stall: 'Romans, hear me: I am Francis, I come from Assisi. I want to tell you of the joy I have in my heart. The Pope ordered me to go to the pigs, and I went. I spoke to them, I told them that we are all creatures of God, brothers in Christ, and they listened to me.' – 'Who's he? He's mad. Look at the way he's dressed.

What's he talking about – Christ? God? The Pope? He stinks! Go away, blasphemer!' – 'No, brothers, sellers and buyers! Stop your selling and buying for a moment! The Pope told me...' – 'He's mad... talking about the Pope! Go away!' – 'No, wait, listen to me... God... no, wait!' One man picks up a stone and throws it at Francis and it hits him in the eye: 'Ow! All right! I understand, today is not the day!' He gets down from the stall and leaves the market square with his brothers.

They pass through the great door in the city wall and find themselves in the fields. It's almost sunset and Francis's companions, exhausted as they are, drop to the ground and fall fast asleep. Francis stands under a huge tree – it's enormous, with a lot of branches, full of leaves, and little birds hopping and chirping, flying around looking for a good place to spend the night. Francis looks at them: 'Oh, birds, how blissful you are, what a marvel! So light you are, and overflowing with joy, you don't have a care and you fly, flapping your wings in the wind, in the air, so easily and in harmony. In the air which

is so close to God that surely it is His very breath...
perhaps the breeze itself is God... and the wind...
and God raises you with His hands and makes you
fly!' While Francis is speaking the words of this
prayer, many other birds arrive from all around,
birds of all kinds: finches, crows and hawks, even
buzzards and eagles from the mountains and
birds from the sea and the rivers. The tree fills up
with birds – so many that you can't see a single
leaf – and they all listen: 'Oh, blissful birds, who
are free and light, who live without possessions,
with no burdens to weigh you down and no power
to enslave you! Oh, if men too could be so light,
without any loads crushing us – men who brag,
full of greed, and thirst for possessions, and desire
for glory; crazed to the point of overpowering each
other, clambering on other people's heads in order
to appear bigger and taller than everybody else –
lies! Rogueries! Wickedness and lack of love! Oh,
if we could free ourselves from this burden, be
stripped of this wretched passion, we could be so
light as to levitate up into the sky, and the puff of a
child would be enough to make us fly!' While still

speaking, Francis turns slightly and notices that, on the wide road behind him, a crowd of people are listening to him. There are women crying; men holding their breath, unable to applaud. And Francis looks up at the sky and says: 'How strange this world is! To make people listen to you, you must speak to the birds!'

FRANCIS IS GOING TO DIE

Saint Francis is now forty-odd years old, but he looks like a decrepit old man. He's got all the diseases you can think of – pains in the stomach, a bad liver, tears of blood in his eyes, trembling marsh fever – but he never stops, he never rests. His brothers reproach him: 'Francis, stop! With all the illnesses you have, you ought to take a break! You cannot risk dropping dead!' But, no, he needs to go on working! If there is a hurricane, which blows down the wheat or the spelt, he goes down to the fields to help the peasants with the harvest; or if a fire burns through the woods, he runs to help the desperate ones. He says: 'No, I can't stop, I must go and earn the alms they give me. Get it into your head that we cannot be maintained by the peasants and those who scrape a living! Do not be afraid to labour with your arms and back. We can't expect these poor people to slog for us just because we say our prayers well and chant glory to God for them too. We can't do nothing but sing while they do nothing but grind away…' He wants to go down to the fields every day but he can't because his back won't hold him up any more, and his eyes are getting worse and worse – so much so that one day they find him in the field, unconscious. At this point the brothers decide to take Francis to a famous doctor. One says: 'There lives in Gubbio a healer, a magister at the university…!' So they set off for Gubbio, carrying Francis on their backs, as he is almost unable to walk…

When they arrive at this doctor's, he, the master, bursts out: 'Oh, brothers, why did you wait so long? Look at the state this poor fellow is in! I must cauterize him!' The brothers ask: 'Cauterize? What does that mean?' – 'I must burn the infection with fire; I need to take a piece of iron, make it red-hot, and burn the temples near the eyes so as to remove the infected matter!' Immediately one of the brothers faints. Another one flees in terror. Meanwhile, the surgeon has plunged the iron into the fire. Francis murmurs: 'Brother Fire… be good, don't make me cry out with pain, be gentle, please, do not harm me too much!' At once the doctor puts the hot iron to the sides of his eyes – you can see the smoke coming out and the smell of burning spreads all around. Francis clenches his teeth, he trembles, he stamps his feet, but he doesn't scream – he resists! In the end he is so pale that he seems bloodless. Then the brothers take him on their shoulders and carry him away.

For two or three days it seems Francis is feeling better, then he starts bleeding again. The brothers make a decision: 'We must go to Siena, where there is a hospital that has the best doctors in the world. It's a long walk, but we must do it.' They prepare a stretcher made with two wooden bars and a blanket. Four of them pick him up and off they go. They walk along the Trasimeno Lake, till they arrive near Stranziano. It's here that Francis says: 'I know this place; close to here is the spring of Bagno Rapo. It's a warm sweet spring, where we swam naked once. Do you mind making a detour to go there? Look over there – you can see the vapour rising.' – 'Yes, yes, Francis, we'll take you over there.'

As they approach the baths the brothers begin to disrobe, but when they come close to the big pool, they see – the warm spring isn't there anymore! It has been covered; hidden with a cupola like a cathedral, with columns and arches, and steam is escaping from the top. 'What has happened?!' – 'Ah, the Earl of Gera stole it!' – says a nearby peasant – 'The spring has always belonged to the city and the community, but he said: "It's mine", and had this cupola built over it like a lid so that nobody else could go in. Only he and his friends can splash around in it, naked: everyone else: "stay out!"' – 'But this is a roguery never seen before!' – cry the friars – 'The people should stick up for their rights! A delegation should go to the Bishop! You must revolt!' – 'Calm down, brothers,' – says Francis, in a feeble voice – 'Do you want to start a war over a splutter of warm water? Be nice! We will find another spring along the road. Pick up your clothes and let's go!' So, half-heartedly, the friars take to the road again.

Step after step after step; and finally they arrive

in Siena without coming across another spring. Just outside the town walls, they run into a multitude of friars coming from every direction. They have found out that Francis is in town and they have all come to meet and embrace him. 'Brothers, be gentle,' – Francis says – 'because, with this love of yours, you risk tearing me to pieces!' Even the wise, skilful doctors have come to meet him and they take him to the hospital. Once there, they cover him with plasters; they put red-hot cups on his chest to bring out all the toxic dampness from his body; they even stick some kind of worms called leeches on his back – little bloodsuckers! But Francis shows no sign of improvement. In the evenings, at sunset, Francis is called by his brothers to take a rest and make himself comfortable among them in a big meadow. They are there to discuss variations on the Rule; to adjust it because, as it is, the Pope and his Ministers don't like it. The first point they discuss is the question of deleting from the Rule the obligation to work to earn their living and be worthy of alms. The friars all begin expounding their own ideas in gentle voices but, as the discussion warms up, they are soon shouting at each other in such cruel terms that it seems strange that they don't all set about swearing! Francis listens – just listens – and never says a word. Only once does he speak: 'That's it! If things go on like this – a gloss here, a compromise there – our Rule will become so sweet, so toned down, that even Venetian merchants will love it!'

Every day the doctors apply a new poultice to Francis but none of the medications bring about any improvement. It's all just pointless torture. Soon Francis realises that these medications aren't working at all: 'Please, brothers, take me home. I feel as if life is leaving my heart.' – 'Sure, Francis, we'll take you home.'

The brothers lift him up again on the stretcher and set off back down the same road that they had come on. Again they pass near the spring but, when they approach it, they see – the cupola and the columns are no longer there! Instead they see, all around on the ground, stumps of columns knocked over, broken arches and splinters of the cupola. And, in the middle of this mess – the spring! Open-air! All free again! The brothers cry: 'What has happened?' – 'Soon after you left,' – says another local peasant – 'a tempest broke out, then there was an earthquake, then – ZAM! – a bolt of lightning struck the cupola and everything was flung up in the air like a volcano spitting lava.' – 'Hurrah, hurrah!' – the friars shout for joy, jumping and dancing – 'It was God – God! – who sent this punishment against those cunning thieves! God! Thank you, God…!' Francis claps his hands trying to get attention. His voice is so weak now that no one can hear him, so he waits for silence, then he says: 'Enough now! Do you really think that, with all the worries that the Eternal Father has in the universe – stars blowing up, comets leaving their paths, planets jumping out of the firmament – do you think he could ever find the time to punish those who trample on the rules and rights of others; thieves of any kind?: "You despotic nobleman, you have committed foul deeds – take this earthquake together with a tempest! You, Lord of Thieves –

take these lighting bolts along with a downpour! And you, cowardly murderer – take this blaze of fire!" Think: there would never again be a single day with a clear sky! We must just thank Him for what has happened and simply wallow in the water, happy!' They all strip naked; enter the spring; sing; laugh; splash around like children; and, gently, they bathe Francis in the water and he too laughs a little laugh. Then they set off again.

They soon pass through a village. The people there knew Francis would be coming so when they see him arrive, they all run joyfully towards him: 'Francis! Francis, stay here with us! We'll give you a big house for you and your brothers!' – 'I am sorry,' – says Francis – 'I thank you with all my heart, but we must go straight back to Assisi.' Then they pass through another little town and it's the same as before: all the people gather around Francis: 'Oh, sweet Francis, be nice, remain here, gladden us – we'll give you the old castle, all for you!' – 'No, thank you, we can't, they are waiting for us at home. We are late!' Among the brothers there is a young one who has just joined the order, and he asks an older one: 'But why do all these people want Francis to stay here with them?' – 'Because they hope that Francis will die here so they can put up a lovely cathedral. Move on! Move on!' Step by step, they make their way to the plain below Assisi. Francis asks his brothers to accompany him to see the Porziuncola – the little church so loved by Francis – and they are about to take the road when a group of mounted soldiers coming down from Assisi yell: 'Stop, brothers! Don't go that way. We are here to protect Francis. Come with us, quickly! You must take shelter in the town!' – 'Why?' – 'Because there are bandits all around here looking for Francis: they know that he is very ill and they want to capture him and bring him to their own cities so that he will die there and earn that place glory and honour.' And Francis says: 'They want me to die everywhere?! I've got half a mind to play a joke on them and not die at all!' The brothers go with the soldiers up the hill and enter the town.

The Bishop of Assisi, who had known Francis since he was a little child, embraces him and says: 'At last, Francis, you have come home. Come into my palace.' He puts Francis on a big bed in his own room. It is most comfortable, and Francis would like very much to sleep, but the mattress is *too* soft – he sinks into the bed, and tosses and turns: 'Brothers, take me off here... I feel like I'm going to vomit!' They lift him off the bed and lay him on the floor and, with tranquillity, he exclaims: 'Oh, yes! This is the life!' Down below, around the palace, the soldiers of the city take turns being on watch. Also, all around the walls, squads of armed men are on the alert to protect the Saint from being kidnapped. Francis, lying there on the floor, calls his brothers: 'Now, please, all of you, brothers of mine, do me a favour... I am down in the dumps... I am feeling a great sadness... with no strength left in my heart... please, grant me a gift: intone for me a sweet, cheerful song.' – 'A song! Yes, surely, Francis. Which one?' – 'The one that goes: "*Glory to the Lord... for brother Sun*." – 'Oh yes, "The Canticle of Brother Sun". Let's do it! Let's pitch our voices, please.' And they position themselves around Francis: 'You, first voice...' – 'AEOHH!' – 'Good. You go over there. Second voice, please...' – 'AEOOOUU-AHA!' – 'Good, you stay here. Third one – and keep the note – let me hear you...' – 'AEOUH!' – 'That's fine, you stay there. Fourth one...!' – 'AEOOOUHA-GAINGA!' – 'No, no – you go away! Right: AAEEOO UU-AA! Now, let's start!

> All praise be yours, my Lord,
> All glory and honour.
> All blessing be yours, my Lord,
> First through Sir Brother Sun
> Who gives us the day and the light.
> How beautiful he is, how radiant
> In all his splendour!
> Of You, the Highest,
> He bears the likeness
> And the glory...'

The soldiers on guard below the palace hear the singing and comment: 'Hey! The Saint is croaking, but in good spirits!' A priest says: 'It doesn't seem right to me... breaking into merry song when you ought to be preparing yourself for a good death!' The singing continued all night but, truth be known, by this time Francis was no longer up there. In fact, only four friars had remained to sing. As soon as the sun had gone down, the other friars, on Francis's order, had quietly carried him out of the palace. They crossed the city of Assisi via underground tunnels, then walked paths that nobody else knew until they finally arrived at the Porziuncola. It is here that Francis has asked to die. The brothers lie him on the earthen floor and he looks up: the roof is ripped apart; wide open. Francis sees the sky and says: 'What a sky! Sprinkled with stars. What a scenario you have prepared for me! Oh, thank you, my Lord, thank you!' And he begins to sing, in a voice that grows softer, and softer, until it becomes a mere whisper:

> 'All praise be yours, My Lord,
> For our sister Bodily Death
> That no one can escape.

The second death will do us no harm
If we are prepared in spiritual peace.
All praise be yours, My Lord,
For this sweetness
That you give to us
In our last breath.
All praise be yours, My Lord!'

- Finis -

Dario Fo

Dario Fo was born in 1926 in Varese, North Italy, near the shore of Lago Maggiore, where he learned storytelling from his grandfather and fishers and glassblowers. He studied art and architecture at university in Milan, but grew increasingly attracted to the theatre and left his studies to pursue that path.

Since the early 1950s, together with his wife, the actress Franca Rame, Fo has written, produced and performed politically charged, satirical plays for the stage as well as radio and television, typically drawing on medieval or Biblical material; and the tradition of the *Commedia dell'arte*. The pair also set up a series of radical theatre companies, and consciously and effectively reached out to audiences outside the traditionally middle class theatre-going crowds. Though enormously popular with the masses, Fo's plays have, over the years, been censored by the Italian government; denounced as blasphemous by the Vatican for their anticlerical satire; and have earned Fo and Rame opposition from various political groups, chiefly those of the far right.

Now in his 80s and still going strong, Fo is internationally recognised as one of the key cultural figures of the 20th century. In 1997 he was awarded the Nobel Prize for Literature, at which time the Award Committee called him the most performed living playwright in the world. Fo's plays are published in over 50 countries and in more than 30 languages. He is also highly respected as an artist and his paintings and drawings have been exhibited internationally.

Highlights of Fo's career include: *Mistero Buffo* (1969); *Accidental Death of an Anarchist* (1970); *Can't Pay? Won't Pay!* (1974); *Female Parts* (1977); and *Johan Padan and the Discovery of Americas* (1992); *Lu Santo Jullare Françesco* (1999).

Mario Pirovano

'Pirovano is a self-taught actor of great expressive quality. I found him exceptional. He showed a vitality that was all his own, and the energetic inventiveness of a great storyteller' – Dario Fo.

In 1983, Mario Pirovano was living and working in London when he met Dario Fo at a performance of his masterpiece, *Mistero Buffo*. The two men sparked an instant friendship, and, since that time, despite having no theatrical background, Pirovano has acted and/or participated in every single work produced by Fo and Franca Rame, in Italy and internationally; as well as performing works by other authors. Pirovano's uniquely close and long-standing personal and professional relationship with Fo makes him without doubt the playwright's most qualified interpreter.

Pirovano has previously translated Fo's *Johan Padan and the Discovery of America* into English for the stage (2002).

Acknowledgements

I would like to thank, with all my heart, my dearest friends professor Judith A. Evans and Rory Stuart, who read through my translation with great care.

I also wish to thank David Grant, who believed in me and supported me from the very beginning; Dominic Selwood, for all his encouragement; Anthony Nott, for his passion and extraordinary dedication in editing this book; my publisher, Simon Petherick, for trusting in me and my work; and Jonathan Salisbury, who made it possible for my translation to become a stage production in the UK.

Finally, I would like to express my deepest gratitude and affection for my Masters, Dario Fo and Franca Rame, who have stood beside me throughout.

Mario Pirovano

**Beautiful
Books**